LOVE IN A SEEDY MOTEL ROOM

A NOVELLA

HEIDI STARK

CONTENTS

PROLOGUE

Motels are full of mysteries, most of which are better unseen
and left unrepeated.

To A, F and J. Thank you for everything. HS xo

1

NOT QUITE A MEET-CUTE

I woke up, completely disoriented, having no idea where I was or how I got there. Judging by there being some sort of fabric covering me, I was in a bed. A cheap hotel bed, I'd guess from the rough, thin texture of the threadbare sheets that covered my body. Groggy, I cautiously opened one eye, concerned about what I was about to see. And I had every reason to be worried. It was dark, and my eyes were having a little trouble adjusting, but I could make out the edges of various surfaces.

My head was pounding, and my mouth was very dry. Despite the darkness, I reached out to the bedside table in hopes Past Me had looked out for Current Me and placed a nice cold bottle of water there for when I woke up. But my attempt was futile, because Past Me was also known as Impulsive Me, and only gave a shit about herself and being in the moment. I knew that for a fact.

While I tried to get my bearings, I suddenly became aware that next to me, a figure lay in the bed. I couldn't see their face in the dark room, and they appeared to be facing the other way. My heart began to pound, adrenalin flooding my body. *Shit*, I thought. *Not again. Who have I woken up next to this time?*

Peering over the dark form, trying to get a better view, I assessed their shape and size. They were slightly smaller than me, from the looks of it, and seemed to have long hair.

Through the darkness, my eyes were beginning to adjust, and I noticed a distinctive rose tattoo at the top of their left shoulder.

I breathed a sigh of relief as I realized it was my good friend Lacey. Relief pounded in my chest. I shock her shoulder.

'Oi, Sasha. Wake up.'

She groaned. 'What? What time is it?'

I flicked on the light beside the bed, which dimly illuminated the cheap hotel room surrounding us. I propped myself up onto my elbows, my arms on top of the sheets exposing my full-length sleeve tattoos.

'What happened last night? And where the fuck are we?'

'You don't remember? And it's a hotel, duh.'

'No shit it's a hotel. And no, I don't remember a fucking thing. Did we...?'

'We did lots of things, speaking of fucking.' Sasha licked her lips.

'Really? Again? What things?' This wasn't the first time I'd received news about my behaviour the night before.

'All of the things. It started with a bath, and things kind of escalated from there.'

That mention of the bath triggered fragments of memories to reform in my brain. While my recollection was mainly a big gap, little slivers began to take shape. I remembered the bath having bubbles, there being champagne, laughing, and touching—lots of touching.

I also remembered a man.

'Did we... I mean, was there—'

'Shit, there was a guy here last night, wasn't there?'

'Who was he?'

'And where is he now? Is our stuff still here? Shit!'

Panicked, we looked at each other. We slowly made our way to the edge of the bed and peered over. I squinted my eyes and cracked one open again, just in case I saw something I needed to try and un-see. There, in front of us, lay a body.

Completely naked. It was a man. We both gasped simultaneously. He was handcuffed to the bench at the foot of the bed.

'Lacey, what did we do?! Did we kill someone?'

She reached out with the newspaper that sat atop the bench and poked at him.

'What are you doing?!' I whispered.

'Seeing if he's alive,' she said, as if this was something she did every day. No response at the first poke with the newspaper, so she jabbed at him again. The naked man groaned in his sleep, and moved slightly. We sat back in the bed, pleased that we didn't have a dead body to deal with.

'Thank fuck for that,' she said. 'I love you, but I don't need to go back to prison with you. I've had enough of that to last me at least ten years.'

I laughed. 'Wouldn't that be something? Back again in there with you, for murdering some naked guy in a seedy motel room? Dodged that bullet this time around. We should probably consider partying a little less next time.' We grinned at each other, knowing that was unlikely to happen. We enjoyed it too much.

'What do you remember from last night, anyway? You seem to have a better recollection than me. I literally remember nothing from the time we headed out to Nate's.' Nate's Bar was the local dive bar, a real hole in the wall with regulars that didn't mess around. It was where some of the best nights were known for starting. But you had to have your wits about you as much as you could be expected to when alcohol was involved; there were always fairly shady characters trying to run scams on unsuspecting patrons; sometimes the shady characters were us.

'Well, you had decided you really, really wanted to get in the bathtub. You wanted a bubble bath, a big foamy frothy luscious bubble bath. I tried to convince you to just watch TV or something easier, but you were absolutely set on it. And you were clearly feeling a bit frisky, you made that very clear.'

This type of behaviour was not unheard of for me, and I was curious to hear what else Lacey remembered.

'What happened next?'

'You peeled your clothes off and jumped in, and invited me to join you.'

'And then?'

'We lathered each other up with soap, rubbing each other all over, into every crevice.

Once we were very clean, we got out of the bath and toweled each other off, very slowly and carefully, once again ensuring that we hit every spot.

Then we came out here and lay down on the bed. You insisted upon exploring my body to make sure I was clean. Where you had any doubts, you made use of your tongue to clean me all over again. You really don't remember any of this?'

'I really don't,' I said. 'Although it sounds like a fun time.'

Lacey laughed. 'It totally was, I hope you get your memory back.'

'Me too. But what about this guy? Where did he come from, and why is he handcuffed to the end of the bed?'

He groaned again, in his sleep, as if he was trying to answer us in his dreams. I noticed that a third champagne glass sat on the table in the corner of the room, presumably his.

'Well, to be honest, I only remember the first part of the night. I'm not sure who this person is or how he fits in. I think I remember him laughing or talking or... I don't know... I guess I just remember that he was here. But he's naked, and he's wearing handcuffs. Don't you have a pair?'

'Yes, you know I do. I've used them on you before, more than once,' I said, winking at her. 'But mine are pink and fluffy ones and these look rather... official.' They were made of some type of silver metal, as you'd expect, and looked very industrial like something you'd see attached to a cop's belt.

Not like the pink fluffy ones with the bogus locks that you'd find down at the local adult shop.

'You're right. These do look like the real deal.'

'Well, we can't just leave him here, passed out like that. And we need to check out soon. The housekeeping staff are going to find him in here.'

'Can we just put some pants on him, to protect their eyes, and leave? He seems alright but what if he's not. I think we should get out of here as soon as we can. I don't want people coming around and asking questions.'

I took another look at the guy, lying there. It felt rude to leave him in this state, helpless, even if we were able to find some pants and pull them up to protect his modesty a bit. 'Let's at least take a look around to see if we can find a key,' I said. Lacey agreed.

We scoured the hotel room, checking in the drawers in the bedside table, the dresser, even the mini-fridge that sat below the wet bar. No luck. We checked under the bed, in the bible inside the drawers, and rummaged through our purses, but couldn't see any sign of a key.

Lacey then checked the bathroom and I was startled when she yelled, 'Bingo! Found it!'

She emerged from the adjacent room, triumphantly holding a tiny silver key.

'Where'd you find it?' I asked.

'There was a whiskey bottle beside the bath and it was in there, right at the bottom. I had to take a swig or two to get it out. Took one for the team, I did. I'm a real trooper!'

I laughed and shook my head. Typical Lacey.

'Save me any? Maybe I need some hair of the dog.'

'Nah, sorry. All gone. Reward for finding the key.' Lacey had to be reminded to share sometimes, especially when it came to alcohol and men.

Speaking of which, we looked over at the man who was still inexplicably sleeping, naked, in our hotel room.

'Wait... what if he's dangerous? He might be a serial killer for all we know?' I felt paranoia creeping in my skull, realising we didn't know this man nor his intentions, especially given Lacey and I had woken up naked in bed together with him in the room.

'A serial killer that in our drunken state we managed to handcuff naked to a bed in a strange hotel room? Not a very good one, if that's the case.'

'What if someone else put him here? What if he's done something bad and we're being framed somehow?'

Lacey looked at me and rolled her eyes in amusement. 'You've been reading those mystery novels again, haven't you!'

'Maybe,' I admitted begrudgingly. She knew me too well. I couldn't get enough of those things, downloaded them all the time and binge-read them whenever I had a spare moment. I supposed it was pretty cool we had woken up to find ourselves right inside a real-life one, a mystery man in our mystery room. I hoped, however, this story featured an ending happier than the ones in the books I tended to read.

'Yeah, well it shows,' she said. 'I say we free him. See if he's a creep. If so, we send him on the way and hightail it out of here. If not, maybe we take him for a coffee at the diner down the street and see if the three of us can piece the night back together. As a team.'

'The naked stranger has joined our team now?' This was a new one, even for us.

'I mean, potentially. Look at him, he's very attractive.'

Lacey had a point. I'd been so concerned about why I couldn't remember the events of last night, and why there was a strange man handcuffed in our hotel room that I hadn't taken a moment to fully inspect him. I let my gaze travel over his body, top to bottom, as he lay there sleeping. He was, in fact, extremely attractive. His eyes were closed, but the rest of his face was angular, with a chiselled jaw and an attractive nose. He had closely-cut brown hair that looked like it had recently been shaved. It was his body that really drew my attention, though. He had broad, muscular shoulders and well-built arms. He clearly worked out. Although he was laying on his side I could make out washboard abs, and a little snail trail of hair and extended downward. And oh my. Whether he was a grower or a shower, he was certainly starting from an impressive place.

'Sasha, stop staring at his schlong! You don't even know the man and you're eyeing it up the way you look at custard squares.'

I looked at her primly. 'I don't know what you're talking about. I was merely assessing the threat in this room.'

'The threat?'

'Yes, this mysterious man who we don't know anything about.'

'And?'

'He gets the all clear so far. A big A-okay from me.'

'Don't you mean a big D-okay?'

'I sure do,' I said. We both laughed and took one more peek at his nakedness before making a move to get up.

I really need to stop doing this shit, I thought to myself. This isn't the first time I've woken up in a strange place, next to someone I don't remember being with. Luckily, this time it was a cheap and dingy hotel room rather than some of the more dangerous places I've found myself on various occasions. However, this is the first time I've woken with a man handcuffed to anything except maybe a headboard once or twice, and I remember those occasions well.

My head still throbbed painfully, no doubt from the copious amount of whiskeys and other substances I'd ingested that had contributed to my memory loss. I really needed to do something about my lifestyle choices. But I always told myself that. And here I was.

I wasn't upset that Lacey and I had carried on intimately. It certainly wasn't the first time. We had originally met when we were in prison, both having made our money slinging drugs on the outside, and running various other scams to support our lifestyle. We quickly formed a bond, in a tough unit with a cliquey group of women that sometimes tolerated us, and other times left us feeling incredibly excluded. Our quick friendship soon turned into something more. We referred to ourselves as prison wives, even having a little ceremony with a selection of our closest fellow inmates. Sharing a bunk bed was a regular occurrence. From that point, we were somewhat stuck together.

Once we got to the outside, our friendship continued but the intimate part of our relationship faded away. There was a whole new world to explore, after all; mainly men. This had caused some initial jealousy, each of us having our moment of 'what if' our relationship could continue on the outside, but we'd got to the point where we'd decided we were better off as friends. For the most part. Largely in part due to the way I enjoyed the touch of a man, their roughness, their gruffness, their edges. And their ability to keep me financially insecure in a world and at a time where that was exceedingly difficult.

That said, every now and then, we'd find our way back to each other in a physical sense. Usually, like last night, it was after hours of wild partying when we'd committed to staying by each other's side for the rest of the night, for better or worse. We would intend on sharing the same bed, and we knew each other so intimately that there was no shyness about sleeping naked. Personally, if there's an attractive person lying beside me in bed naked, I'm going to end up reaching out and touching them and I haven't encountered anyone who has ever not felt the same way. Neither of us saw anything wrong with a friends-with-benefits type arrangement here and there. All very low-key, nothing serious.

Despite the casualness of our physical relationship at the moment, there were times that I'd long for Lacey's touch, the softness of her hands, the warmth of her mouth on my body. And while I appreciated the hard angles and dominance and control that a very masculine man could bring to the table, and to the bedroom, sometimes I found myself craving her. Lacey tended to have moments like this herself, her feelings for me often seeming more intense than mine for her. Personally, I tried to push those types of emotions down and focus on other things as much as possible; it seemed better that way. Like now, for instance, it seemed more pressing to figure out who this well-endowed man was at the end of our bed.

I stood up, stretching and feeling all of the cricks in my neck and shoulders that come from a wild night out in one's thirties. 'Jesus, I feel like I lifted weights all night or something. What on earth did we do when we left the bar?'

Lacey laughed. 'You really remember nothing about the evening do you.'

I shook my head.

'We went to Nate's Bar for a while, and then visited Randy's tattoo shop.'

'Oh shit—,' I ran into the bathroom to look at myself in the mirror. 'I didn't—?'

'No, but you were thinking about it.'

I was fairly well covered in tattoos, most of them from the outside and a couple from my time in prison. It wasn't unheard of for me to get a wild idea to get another one while I was heavily intoxicated. But fortunately, it appeared that last night I didn't have any needles anywhere near me. I breathed a sigh of relief.

'Oh, good. I'm running out of room. Need to be picky about what I have and where. I have it all planned out.'

Lacey laughed. 'You're a work of art, that's for sure.'

I pulled on my panties and a bra, which were crumpled beside the bathtub, which made sense given what Lacey had shared about what transpired last night. I noticed that my top and jeans were located nearby, both inside out as if they'd been pulled off in a rush, or maybe in a fit of passion. Perhaps both. I turned them both back the right way and put them on. I looked over at Lacey, who was pulling on her own T-shirt and leggings. She rarely wore underwear. Her breasts were small enough to not require a bra, and I knew she preferred not to wear panties.

Both dressed, it was time to figure this out. 'Do we wake him?' I asked.

'I think we need to at this point.

'Should we keep him handcuffed?'

'Yeah, I mean that seems safer at this point. That way, he can't try any funny business. Once we've established he's not a threat, we can talk about releasing him. Otherwise, he'll still be here when the maid comes in to clean the room.'

I laughed, picturing a room attendant's shocked face were they to come into the room to find a naked man inexplicably cuffed to a bench at the end of the bed. Glancing around this low-rent hotel room, I was fairly certain anyone working here had seen much worse.

We approached him, from each side, and crouched down beside him. I reached out and touched his shoulder, shaking it gently. He moaned but didn't wake.

More firmly, I shook his shoulder and said, 'Oi, wake up!'

He moaned again and this time, as I had, opened one eye and squinted against the dim light that was now emanating from the bedside lamp. 'What... what happened? Where am I? What am I doing here?'

'These are life's important questions. But for now, we have some questions for you. Who are you?'

The naked man, apparently not realising he'd been restrained, made a move to sit himself up using his handcuffed wrist. Noticing he was unable to move freely, he glanced down at his arm and said, 'What the hell? Why am I handcuffed? Let me go!' He tried to pull away from the bench, but it was fairly sturdy and utilitarian, just like everything else in this seedy accommodation.

'Stop asking questions,' said Lacey. 'And start answering.' Her voice was low and she spoke slowly and directly. 'If you don't want to spend the rest of goodness knows how long, handcuffed to this bench, you will answer our questions.'

I liked it when she exerted control, finding myself a little turned on. I think it's because I remembered a few times that she'd exerted dominance over me. They had been fun times.

'Rob,' he said. 'My name is Rob.'

'Rob what?'

'Rob... Smith.'

'No it's not. You hesitated. What's your actual last name.'

He looked at us both. 'Baker. Rob Baker.'

'You're lying to us,' Lacey hissed, moving threateningly towards him.

Rob sighed. 'Okay look, it's Rob Fortner. Assuming those are my jeans over there, and they look like it, there should be an ID in the pocket.'

I walked over to the jeans that were crumpled in the floor and nudged at them with my foot, as if to make sure they were safe. They did appear to be heavier than a pair of pants should be. I picked them up and reached into a pocket, pulling out a wallet with an ID that confirmed he was indeed, Rob Fortner, age 38, from Boise, Idaho.

'Idaho, aye?' I said. 'What are you doing all the way out here?'

'Visiting family. And being handcuffed to benches in grimy hotel rooms, apparently.' He had a sense of humor. That was a start.

'What are you doing here? Why are you in this room?'

'You don't know?'

'We wouldn't be asking you if we didn't know.' Lacey was getting irritated, as she quickly tended to do. She nudged him with an outstretched toe. 'Tell us what you're doing here, why you're here. Stop mucking us around.'

He looked at us with what appeared to be honest eyes, and goodness knew I was fairly good at picking out the liars. 'I truly don't know.'

'I think he's telling us the truth, Lace,' I said.

She narrowed her eyes, looking once again at the naked man.' What are you going to do if we release you from these handcuffs, Rob Fortner from Boise, Idaho? Can we trust you?'

'I'll do whatever you want, I swear. I just want to get up and go. Put my pants on, first. Preferably, if you will let me.'

'Fine. But if you try anything we're going to beat the shit out of you and leave your body here for the next cleaning person to find.' He looked at Lacey like she was a madwoman, which to be fair wasn't a far stretch. He wasn't the first one to look at her that way, both in and outside of prison.

'I get that message loud and clear. I don't want any trouble. Just let me grab my things and I'll be out of your way.'

I raised an eyebrow at Lacey and she nodded. I picked up the small metal key that we'd placed on the table in the corner and used it to unlock the handcuffs that were clamped around Rob's wrist. After a couple of wiggles, the clasp sprang free and he quickly removed his hand, shaking it to get some movement and blood flow back. They had been secured fairly tightly.

Rob stood up and proceeded to put on his jeans and, looking around the immediate area, found his crumpled T-shirt nearby. He pulled that on as well.

He looked at me. 'Wallet?'

Lacey and I glanced at each other. It was tempting to take his wallet and get him to leave without it. When glancing at his ID earlier, it looked like he had a little bit of cash, maybe forty bucks. That wouldn't get us far, but it did suggest he had some type of access to money, which could be useful later.

'Okay but first, I have an idea,' I said. 'There's a diner down the street. Let's go, you're buying.' May as well get him to spend that forty dollars on us, and maybe get to the bottom of this little mystery of ours, I thought.

Lacey and I picked up any other personal items we could find; for me, that really only included our purses and my lipstick which I appeared to have thrown across the room while I was drunk. The only other things that didn't seem to belong to the hotel were the empty bottles of various liquor that we'd made our way through the night before. Wouldn't be needing those. *Probably didn't need so many of them last night, either*, I thought wryly, my head still pounding.

The diner was a bit grungy, if a dive diner was a thing this was it. But the tables were clean enough. The lighting was fairly dim, and an old school juke box sat in the corner, taking up a massive amount of room to crank out tunes that nobody had heard in years. Next to the cashier, a long low breakfast bar with low stools extended the length of the diner. Lining the windows were a long row of booths, the chairs upholstered in vinyl and the tables topped with a faux vintage linoleum. Or based on the looks of this diner, probably was the original thing. We took a seat at one of the booths a few tables in from the door, Rob sitting opposite the two of us.

The waitress brought over three large menus, the kind that are lined with fabric and covered in a plastic coating, with flecks of baked-on egg and grubby fingerprints. 'Coffee?' She asked. 'Yes, three please,' said Lacey, not giving Rob a choice. She returned promptly with a carafe of hot coffee and three mugs, and poured a generous quantity of the steaming brown liquid into each. The scent of coffee assaulted my nostrils in the best way, giving me the first vestiges of life after such a rough night out. I brought the mug to my lips and inhaled the bold scent of coffee that was going to help take care of this pounding headache.

We perused the menu and when the waitress returned and asked if we wanted any food, Lacey spoke up first. Three eggs, over hard, with some bacon and sausage. And a side of toast with jam. Oh, and a pancake side as well. My eyes grew large, perceptible perhaps only to Lacey. Rob glanced at her, too. She shrugged and said, 'What, I'm hungry.' The waitress looked at me next and I asked for some bacon and eggs with buttered toast. Rob ordered the steak and eggs. *Mmm, a man that likes meat. Sexy*, I thought.

After breakfast, and lots of hungover chit-chat about a range of topics from whether alien life exists to the origin of chili fries, Lacey attempted to convince Rob that we should all go back to his apartment to hang out. The truth was, she couldn't bear to go back to her shithole of an apartment that she was renting a room in, and I didn't really have anywhere else to go either. She also likely wanted to see if he had anything valuable that he could pinch when he wasn't looking. These two factors ensured that she was at her most persuasive.

"Come on, we can stop by the grocery store. I'll make us food."

"We just ate," he laughed.

"Oh come on, it will be fun! Snacks then. Movie and snack day with your new friends!" Rob seemed hesitant, and for good reason knowing how Lacey could be when she got into a stranger's home. It was like he sensed that about her, that she wasn't always someone who should be trusted by a stranger. Eventually, and somewhat reluctantly, he sighed in resignation and said, "Fine, let's all go back to mine. I wasn't expecting company so don't judge me for the mess. Let's call an Uber."

"Wait, do you have roommates?" Lacey suddenly thought to ask.

"No, it's just me at the moment. My roommate moved out last month, he went overseas for work. I'm in the process of searching for another one, but it's been nice having the place to myself." I noticed Lacey watching him as he spoke, seeming to absorb the information and craft a few potential scenarios that could unfold when we got to his place. I knew how her mind worked, and she was thinking about all kinds of mischief.

The Uber dropped us off in a pleasant blue-collar neighbourhood over on the other side of town. His apartment was nice, surprisingly large. It featured a sizeable open plan living room with a kitchen at the rear. The walls were partially exposed brick, giving it a loft feel I'd only seen in magazines. I wondered how much rent he was paying for the place. He had a bike standing against the wall near the entrance, which opened into an open plan living room and kitchen setup. A large screen TV sat on top of a pretty nice entertainment unit that contained a gaming system and what appeared to be a DVD player. *How very old school of him*, I thought.

Rob showed us around. Lacey was very interested in what the place had to offer, picking up trinkets and examining them closely, probably to see what they might be worth were she to resell them. "Lacey, stop it!" I hissed at her, when she started nosing around in drawers when she thought Rob wasn't looking.

"She's fine," said Rob, laughing as he overheard me. "If I was in a strange man's apartment I'd be trying to figure out what his gig was. Especially given the way we uh.. met." We all looked at each other and, after a moment of silence, laughed at the reality of our first meeting.

Rob showed us around the kitchen. "Help yourself to anything you like. Fridge has some cold beer, and here's my little bar setup," he said, gesturing to an area of the counter with an array of liquor bottles. "There are snacks in this cupboard, too," he said, pointing to a cupboard beside the fridge. He opened it briefly, giving us a brief view of pretzels and chips. Lacey immediately headed over and grabbed a bag of pretzels. She was like a bottomless pit, always hungry. But she was used to not being certain where her next meal was coming from, so it made sense that she would stock up when she could. Heck, I'd be surprised if she didn't put the rest of the snacks in her oversized purse when Rob wasn't looking.

I noticed that there were dirty glasses, cups and plates stacked in and around the sink.

Still way tidier than my place, I thought. Domestic cleanliness was not my strong suit, despite having worked as a hotel housekeeper myself for a while. Somehow, I found that it was much easier to organise other people's lives than my own.

We sat down on the couch and Rob handed Lacey the remote. She'd mentioned a few shows that she'd been wanting to watch and she oriented herself with his cable setup and put something on. "It's trash but I love it," she said, "and this guy cracks me up". She pointed to the screen, and it was her favourite character on a well-known reality show. "Is this one of those shows where they all argue and scream at each other?" asked Rob.

"Sure is," said Lacey, happily.

We watched for a while, and partway through I decided to pour myself a drink. It was hard to resist a fairly well-stocked bar like his, and I was a sucker for a good whiskey. I walked over to the bar and grabbed a bottle of whiskey, and then a glass located by the sink. Rob appeared by my side. 'Let me at least get you a clean glass,' he said. He handed one to me and his hand brushed against mine. I felt a little zip of electricity. He was very attractive, after all. I made eye contact and could see he was returning my gaze; I guessed that perhaps he was a little interested in me as well. I smiled at him, and returned to the couch.

We spent the rest of the afternoon watching movies and enjoying drinks and snacks. Every now and then one of us would laugh at something that happened in a scene, but for the most part we just sat there, relaxed, as if we were old friends. I mean, Lacey and I technically were, but there was a relaxed camaraderie between the three of us, even though Rob was a new friend and this was the first time Lacey and I had been in his apartment.

At some point, I went to get a glass of water and could feel his presence as he also got up and moved over to where I stood. I felt him press up behind me. He leant over my shoulder and I could feel his breath on my ear. The little hairs on my neck bristled at his breath. He reached around, placed his hands on my forearms just for a second. I could have sworn I felt a hardness forming in his pants as he gently made contact with me from behind, but just as quickly as he appeared, he pulled back. 'Could you pour me a glass while you're at it? I'm thirsty, too.'

Lacey went off to use the restroom at one stage, leaving us on the couch in the living room by ourselves. He leaned in and kissed me, the electricity hanging thick in the air between us. It was the kind of kiss that hung heavy with promise and undone acts, immediately making me crave more. I reached over to place my hand on his leg and noticed the tightness of his pants. This was an interesting development. One that I was very interested in, even though—and maybe in some ways, because—things seemed to be happening very quickly. We heard Lacey heading back to the living room and quickly distanced ourselves, him hoping up from the couch and facing away so she couldn't see the impressive bulge that had formed. Once she'd passed, he headed off in the opposite direction, saying he was going to check on something in the other room.

'We should take some of his stuff. That bike looks pretty good. I think we could get a few hundred for it at least, but it's a bit big. And that gaming system is top of the range.' Lacey scanned the room with interest, her expert eye locking in like a missile on anything of potential resale value. She was a pro at assessing how much she could likely pawn something off for, and could estimate with incredible accuracy just about in her sleep.

When I'd first taken a look around the apartment, I'd immediately become concerned that this was where Lacey's mind would go. That's to say, mine would have headed further in the same direction had I not started to develop a slight carnal interest in our new friend, Rob. We'd certainly helped ourselves to belongings in a number of men's apartments over the years. But those were men that we never intended to see again. And maybe that's how Rob was intended to be from Lacey's perspective. But I wasn't so sure, I had been enjoying his company—at least for now. If he pissed us off or gave reason for us to be worried, I was open to changing my mind.

'Let's just cool it for now,' I said to Lacey. 'Relax, watch some shows, enjoy the moment. It's safe here and quite peaceful. If we take his shit we have to leave and find some place to go.'

Lacey realized I was right and nodded, sitting back on the couch and relaxing while she munched on pretzels. Rob returned from the other room, none the wiser that we'd been discussing hawking all his belongings at one of the local pawn shops that recognised both Lacey and me as regulars.

At some point after the evening had arrived, Lacey fell asleep and she began to snore softly. Rob got up and left the room briefly, returning with a blanket and a pillow. I gently tucked her head onto the pillow and placed the blanket over her. We left the TV on to mask any noise. After the way he had kissed me earlier, and the bulge I had seen forming in his pants, I felt fairly confident that we were going to be making some noise.

I was becoming turned on by Rob's own arousal. He was an attractive man who desired me, and that was something that I found sexy as hell. But I was also conflicted.

'Lacey's sleeping right out there. I don't want to wake her up, she'll be really pissed.' I wasn't just afraid of waking her out of an abundance of courtesy. Lacey had a history of being very jealous, and I don't think she could bear to wake up in this strange apartment, and see me getting fucked by this guy we just met; at least, without inviting her.

'I do have a bedroom, you know. I wasn't suggesting we bang on the ground, and wake her to the noises of the pots and pans clattering all over the place.' A bed did sound awfully good. The one back at my flat was not the most comfortable, some hand-me-down I'd gotten from roommates past. It was a piece of furniture I tried not to think about; the way it had been passed around from housemate to housemate, I had no doubt that it had seen some thinks.   So, yes, his actual bed sounded divine. It had to be better than what I had waiting for me back at home.

'Are you sure you're not some kind of serial killer or ax murderer? Taking me off to your room to have your wicked way with me?'

Rob laughed. 'Well, if I was a serial killer or ax murderer I don't think it would matter if you came to my bedroom or not. I'm sure that I'd find a way to knock you off in the living room. It would probably be easier, actually—the noise from the TV covering up any suspicious sounds.' He had a valid point. 'However, I make no guarantees that I won't have my wicked way with you. In fact, I don't think I'll be able to keep my hands off you when we get in there.' He advanced on me, putting his hand on my chin and tilting it up. He kissed me, right on the mouth and then quickly pulled away, turning his back to me. He started to walk away in the direction of his room. 'So, you coming or not?'

Rob gestured for me to follow him. I smiled and followed his lead. We tiptoed out of the main living room and down the hall to his bedroom. I hadn't poked around in here earlier, but it was nice. A comfy-looking king-sized bed with a comforter, and a large dresser off to the side. A small TV sat on the dresser, as well as some basics like hair gel and deodorant. A few items of clothing were strewn in the corner. I was impressed—for a man, the room was pretty clean, and a shitload cleaner than my own room back at home. It even smelled clean, like a rainforest detergent or some fancy shit like that.I figured either way I would piss somebody off; Lacey, for getting naked with this hot stranger while she slept in the room next door. I could manage that, and would do my best to keep it from her for as long as possible. Or me, missing out on the opportunity to get some action with a hottie who I'd just met. That would result in me being incredibly frustrated and having to put effort into finding some other guy to give me some relief in the next day or two. I decided to back myself on this one, my needs mattered too.

Rob approached me and guided me to the bed, where we sat down next to each other. He looked at me, right in the eyes, and I realized how sexy his own brown eyes were. I could tell that he wanted me, and I felt the same way. He pulled me to him and kissed me tenderly, our mouths interlocking and our tongues exploring. I liked the way he kissed; it gave me tingles and I wanted more.

'We going to do this or what? You've been looking at me all night like a horny teenager.'

'Oh, you noticed? I was trying to be discreet about it,' he laughed.

'Well, you failed big time. The perpetual tightness in your pants has been a dead giveaway.'

He smirked. 'You noticed that, huh? I was trying to be discreet.

'Hard to be discreet with that thing, I imagine.' This conversation was starting to make me feel a little flustered.

'Well, seeing I failed once already today, I'm hoping that the rest of the night won't be a failure.'

'We'll see,' I winked at him, running my hand gently down his forearm, and up his leg to where I could see a prominent bulge was once again forming in his pants.

Feeling emboldened, I proceeded to give him a little bit of a lap dance, as sexy music played in my head. I wasn't sure quite what came over me, but I couldn't help it. The stiffness in his pants grew visibly larger as I gyrated my hips as I straddled him. 'You really know how to move,' he murmured, watching me as if he was hypnotised. 'There are a lot of things I know how to do,' I said, enjoying the connection of our close eye contact and the manly smell of him; clean, but masculine.

He pulled off my T-shirt and caressed my breasts, gently, with his fingertips. 'Oh god, Sasha, you're beautiful.' Nobody had really spoken to me like this before. Usually sex was just a stick-it-in-and-get-it-done type scenario with the men I typically hooked up with. Don't get me wrong—I had no problem with a man dominating me in the bedroom and in fact found it a huge turn-on. But Rob seemed different. Like he was open to giving as well as taking.

He placed me at the foot of the bed, gently lowering me onto it. While we kissed some more, he unbuttoned my jeans, unzipping them and then grabbing hold of them by the waist-band. He lowered them slowly while we continued to make out, leaving my panties on. He pushed me back and leaned on top of me. I could feel his hardness through his underwear and mine. He reached underneath my shirt, running his hand up my bare stomach and calling a tingly, pleasant chill to run throughout my body. His hand landed on my breast, his fingers softly stroking, finding their way to my nipple which was hardening at his touch. I moaned in pleasure; his fingers were a little rough, causing a pleasant friction wherever he placed them on my body. He reached down and pressed his fingers into me, and I moaned as I felt them slide inside me while he continued to kiss me. I figured he was about to put himself inside me and I wasn't against it, but I was enjoying this level of personal attention. The fact he was stopping to use his fingers first was progress from what I'd more recently been accustomed to from a man. It turned out, however, that there was more to come.

He slid himself down my body until his face neared my waist. He then lowered his head between my thighs and began to use his tongue to bring me pleasure. It had been a while since a man had performed this act on me. I'd forgotten how good could feel, his tongue dancing over me, teasing and exciting me. The guys I tended to get intimate with tended not to be the types to do this for their women. But Rob seemed to be only too happy to take care of me in this way. I moaned as he expertly used his mouth to trigger sensations throughout my body that I'd forgotten were possible. He continued to pay intimate attention to me until my pleasure peaked, and I had an intense, euphoric orgasm caused a sensation of exploding tingles to radiate throughout my body. I wrapped my thighs around his head and arched my back as I allowed the pulsating squeezes to flow throughout me and eventually subside. 'You liked that, huh?' He asked.

'I, uh—yes, I very much liked that.'

'Good,' he said. 'That was my intention. And now, if you don't mind, I'd quite like to be inside you, Sasha.'

I nodded and pulled him towards me. He climbed on top of me and I grabbed onto his strong biceps as they framed my face and he began to rub his hardness against my wetness.

As he slid into me, I gasped. Thinking back to the time we first met, when he was naked and handcuffed to the bench in the seedy hotel room, I determined that he indeed was both a shower and a grower. And I was one very lucky lady. We began to make love, slowly at first and then he began to increase his pace. We kissed, tongues exploring each other as he continued to enter me, in and out, over and over again until he came, shuddering, as he pulled himself deeper inside of me. We lay there, sweaty and spent, until finally he pulled out of me.

'Want a bottle of cold water?' He asked, pulling on his pants and kissing me on the nose. 'Oh yes, please. Abso-fuck-ing-lutely,' I replied. He really knew how to please a woman. Making love attentively, followed by an icy cold glass of agua. This was the life. We lay there, enjoying our water while we chatted late until the morning, until right before the sun came up.

I found myself having no difficulty with conversation, which sometimes could be an issue when I was making small talk after sex. Usually, the guys I dated had nothing to talk about other than their work, wrestling and whiskey; and usually the conversations only lasted as long as it took for me to get my clothes on hurriedly and rush out the door, hoping I'd never bump into them again. I could hold conversations on any of those topics with confidence, but it could be tiring talking about the same old thing after a while. With Rob, however, talk flowed smoothly. He had a cheeky way about him, and would tease me if I revealed something scandalous like my love for ridiculous TV game shows. We both supported the same baseball team, and worked out we'd probably attended several of the same games in our city. We talked a little bit about our family and friends, but he seemed to focus on lighter things, which worked for me. I was very guarded about talking about the family members who remained in my life, who were few and far between. And I certainly didn't want to start down any paths that could lead to him finding out that I'd been in prison. That didn't tend to go over well with folks who hadn't been in themselves. So I was very happy to keep things lighthearted. Besides, we hadn't even known each other for 24 hours.

Finally, we fell asleep and I dreamed, which I rarely do. It was a happy dream, infusing actual memories of the past with fantastic sequences where I played atop fluffy clouds and all of my pets came to frolic alongside me. Rob was in the dream as well, which I found surprising when I thought about it. Just met the guy and he was already invading my dreams. Although he'd also invaded my body in the best way; he must have left an impression on me while doing so.

2

WALK OF THE SHAMELESS

I woke up, disoriented again, but this time in a much nicer location than the seedy hotel room where I'd woken the previous day. The sheets felt soft, luxurious and thick across my body, and a cool breeze blew on me from the nearby fan. I got acclimated much more quickly as well; the moment I noticed the figure lying beside me, this one much bigger than me, I recalled everything. Rob, the diner, his apartment, what he'd done to me with his tongue and other body parts the night before. This was a much nicer way to wake up. I rolled over and looked up at him. He was also starting to wake. 'Hey there, sleepyhead. How'd you sleep?'

'Well.' I reflected that it had actually been the best sleep I'd gotten in ages. I felt wonderful, rested and satisfied, from the sleep itself and from the activities we'd engaged in during the night.

'Can I get you a coffee?'

'For someone who doesn't really know me, you know me very well,' I said, laughing. 'Yes, please.' I suddenly remembered my best friend had joined us on this visit to Rob's apartment. 'Oh shit, Lacey's out there as well. I'll come out with you. We can just act casual'.

Lacey looked surprised when she saw us heading out of the hallway leading to his bedroom together. 'What the hell? It's morning, I'm assuming you two went off to fuck or something.

Thanks for the invite.' She sounded annoyed, and I was pretty sure she was only half-joking. I felt a little bit guilty, leaving her out in the living room by herself while Rob and I got to know each other on a whole other level; that said, she was perfectly safe covered in a comfortable blanket with a TV to watch when she woke up. Much more safe and secure than she'd have been if we hadn't stayed here overnight.

I realized my plan to act casual was probably a bit unrealistic. I'm sure we had that deer-in-headlights look like we'd been up to something, both looking a bit disheveled, and both heading out of the hallway from his bedroom at the same time. That would have been a tough thing to explain away. Plus, Lacey was shrewd, a tough-minded criminal after all. It really was hard to put anything past her, she tended to notice things, and to piece things together that normally flew over other people's heads.

"Don't be rude," I said, a bit embarrassed by how direct she was being. "You fell asleep, and we left you to it."

"You didn't just go to sleep though, did you?"

"A lady never tells," I said, Rob and I making eye contact and exchanging a grin.

"I saw that, you dirty fucks. Banging away in the bedroom while I slept here in the next room," she said, raising her voice in agitation. 'And you're the furthest thing from a lady, Sasha. Well except for me that is,' she added. The three of us laughed at her self-aware admission.

'Alright well, we should be going then, Lace. We've got things to do today, we should get out of Rob's hair.'

We grabbed our things, and as predicted Lacey also grabbed the half-eaten bag of pretzels. 'Mind?' She raised an eyebrow at Rob, gesturing towards the bag.

'Not at all, be my guest.'

'Thanks. Oh, should probably have one for the road, too,' she said. She walked over to the bar area and poured herself a hefty helping of whiskey, and downed it in one gulp.

While she was doing this, Rob discreetly handed me his phone and I plugged in my phone number. Lacey didn't seem to notice, or if she did, she didn't let on, preferring to focus on the whiskey.

'Thanks again. Pleasure doing business with you, although the pleasure part was all thanks to Sasha, I'm sure.'

I walked to Rob and gave him a hug, slightly embarrassed at Lacey's shenanigans and mouthed *Sorry* at him. He shrugged and gave me a small wave as we left his apartment. 'Bye now. Be safe out there,' he said.

'What the fuck was that?' Asked Lacey as we made our way out of the apartment complex. 'I wanted to case the joint and instead you end up ditching me for his dick. I hope it was at least good. I might have wanted to check it out for myself. Some friend you are.'

'Lacey, you fell asleep. I didn't want to wake you up, and.. I mean, he was very hot. He was into it, I was into it. One thing led to another and...'

'Oh, please.' Lacey rolled her eyes. 'I was the first one who noticed he was hot, right back in the first place when we saw him at the hotel room. Did you ask me if I might be interested? Or just assume you could take him for yourself?' Lacey frowned and crossed her arms petulantly across her chest.

'Were you interested, Lacey?' I hadn't noticed Lacey showing any signs of physical attraction towards Rob, or even any attempts to flirt. She seemed more interested in his whiskey collection and his snacks, as well as what she could find to watch on TV.

'That's not the point!' She huffed. I figured she was just grumpy in the moment and feeling left out. Lacey had a tendency to get very upset very quickly, and then the same things would blow over very quickly. It was one of her personality quirks that I'd learned to live with.

By now we were standing outside the building, and needed to figure out where each of us was going. 'Okay well, I need to get home and take care of some things.' I knew that if I didn't make a move, Lacey would want to just wander around all day aimlessly, trying to avoid what she might find when she arrived at her temporary 'home', for lack of a better word. I felt a bit guilty, but I did have some things to do around my flat, and I had a shift the next day.

'Can we just hang out for an hour more? I'm trying to wait until things have cleared out back at the group house.'

'Listen, let's order a car and have them take the long way. I'll get them to drop you off after me. That should get you there at a better time.'

'That works,' she said, looking down and absentmindedly kicking at a pebble on the sidewalk.

'Things will get better, Lace. I'm sure of it,' I said.

Lacey looked up at me. 'I hope so,' she said. 'Because they sure as hell can't get much worse.'

I stuck my key in the lock and went through my usual routine of wedging my foot into the doorjamb and pressing my weight against the door handle as I jiggled the key, relieved when I heard the *click!* sound as the lock sprang free. I'd bugged my flat's property manager about it a couple of times, but I could tell they couldn't care less if I was able to get into my tiny little flat or sat outside in the cold all night. Places like mine generated some income for them, but weren't a priority for a company like theirs. I was used to it, and I guess grateful to have a roof over my head. It hadn't always been that way. I headed inside and flicked the light on. It flickered twice and then switched on, brightly illuminating the little studio room. I kicked off my shoes and threw my keys on the small table that jutted out awkwardly into the main space. It was a far cry from Rob's fancy loft, but it did the job when it came to a safe-ish place to eat, sleep and watch TV.

'Sasha!' I heard loud knocking on my door and the familiar sound of my landlord, Eugene. 'I know you're in there! Open up!'

Eugene was a gross man. Overweight, ruddy-faced, kind of perky. Always running around with a wifebeater on that was covered in some sort of stain. I tried to avoid him as much as I possibly could, but he had this ability to be all over the flat complex all the time. I grabbed an envelope out of my purse on the way to the door.

'You're late on rent again, Sasha!' He yelled at me as I opened the door.

'Here you go, Eugene,' I said, thrusting the enveloped at him. 'It's for this month plus what I owed you for last month.'

'Oh, this is new. Saaasha,' he looked me up and down, a smile forming on his greasy face.

'Paying your rent almost on time. Veeery interesting. You got a promotion or something? Make better life choices?' The audacity, I thought, as this grubby man stood there leering at me. Like being the onsite property manager at a shitty complex, covered in spaghetti sauce and leering at women in their homes while demanding payment was the height of life success.

'None of your business, Eugene. You want the money or should I take it back? And while you're at it, for the love of god would you fit his fucking lock?!' He scowled and quickly stuffed the envelope into the waistband of his pants. Talk about gross. I hope he managed his own cashier duties and some poor admin clerk didn't need to put their hands on that. He scurried off, muttering to himself, no doubt preparing to torment the next tenant.

I spent the rest of the day tidying up around my flat and giving it a thorough clean. After picking up some extra shifts at the grocery store, I hadn't had much time to do anything other than work, eat and sleep, so there was a fair amount of vacuuming, dusting and wiping down various surfaces to do; not to mention, several loads of laundry to wash, fold and put away. My cleaning skills left a bit to be desired so it wasn't something I could take care of very quickly, either. A couple of hours in, things were starting to look a lot better and I sat down on the couch with a cold beer to reward my efforts. As I cracked open the can I heard my phone beep. Assuming it was likely Lacey with an update on her living situation, I was surprised and quite pleased to see that it was from Rob. *Hey there, sexy. I had a great night last night. Not trying to sound too keen, but I'm off tonight and wondering if you wanted to come over again. Just you this time xx.*

Well, that was an interesting development. The area between my legs started to throb just reading those words, in anticipation of what would almost certainly happen if I did go over to his place. A repeat certainly sounded enjoyable. I knew that there was lots of advice out there about playing hard to get, about making yourself sound busy. But the thought of the way Rob had used his tongue and his hardness on me last night was fresh in my mind, and instead of playing games I decided to go and take what was on offer. *Sure,* I replied. *I need to get back home tonight, though. Meeting with Lacey first thing and then work. See you around 730.*

3

OPPORTUNITIES AND OBLIGATIONS

I woke up the next morning and was surprised to find that I was still nestled in the nook of his armpit, my right arm dangling over his chest. I was usually a very restless sleeper, and in the odd event I did sleep next to an intimate partner, I had a tendency to kick, toss and turn until we ended up on opposite sides of the bed. Curiously, this didn't seem to be the case with Rob. 'Good morning, sleepyhead,' he said as I lifted my chin to look up at him. He kissed me on the forehead.

'How long have you been awake?'

'Not too long. I didn't want to disturb you, though. It's like when a cat comes and sits on your lap and you don't want to move because it looks so comfortable, you know?'

'You're comparing me to a pet cat?'

'Slightly less furry, from what I saw last night.' He laughed and winked at me. I rolled my eyes and smiled in return.

'I'd better check to make sure, though, if that's alright with you. Make sure I didn't miss anything in a state of delirium or something.' He wiggled out from underneath me and proceeded to lower himself under the covers until his mouth was once again firmly pressed against me. He began pleasuring me with his tongue, slowly, teasingly, and I moaned in pleasure at his touch. A girl could get used to this personalised attention. He continued to work his magic, squeezing my thighs as he focused intently on bringing me to yet another intense orgasm.

He scooted back up and gave me a long, slow kiss. 'Turn over, I want you from behind.' I was more than happy to turn over and position myself on all fours, where he entered me with his girthy hardness. Once again, we made slow, tender love as he held onto my waist. We rocked back and forth, rhythmically, in unison, until I felt his body tense up and he groaned heavily. His body pulsated and then he held me close to him as our hearts slowly returned a more normal beat. He kissed me on the back, and we once lay down next to each other.

He traced the outline of the side of my face furthest from him, as he gazed at me. 'I feel like you might enjoy a coffee. Am I right?'

'You're learning,' I replied, smiling. This man had the knack of earning points with me in a number of ways, I was beginning to find out.

I checked my phone and saw that I had several texts and a missed call. It was Lacey. I looked at my calendar. *Shit*, I thought, realising I was meant to have met with her an hour ago and she was probably still waiting for me. This new relationship, or whatever it was, was really making me distracted, complacent, a bad friend.

So sorry, I texted. *Lost track of time. Be there in 30.*

No reply from Lacey. I bet she was furious at me.

I jumped out of bed and started to quickly get dressed. Rob returned with a coffee as I was pulling on the second leg of my jeans. He looked confused, realising I appeared to be getting ready to leave. 'What, no coffee?'

'I—I'm sorry, I need to go. I have a thing to take care of.'

I yanked on my sweater and grabbed my bag.

'I don't understand. Did I do something wrong?'

'No, I just have to go. I'll text you later.'

I headed to the door, slid on my shoes without untying the laces, and bolted out the door leaving a very confused Rob standing in the bedroom doorway with two steaming mugs of coffee in his hands.

'Where the hell have you been, Sasha?' Lacey was glaring at me as I ran breathlessly into the coffee shop.

'I'm sorry I'm late, Lace. Truly. I lost track of time and I came as soon as I realized.'

'What were you doing to be so late, anyways? You knew how important this was to me!' As anticipated, Lacey was royally annoyed. I'd promised that I'd meet her to go over her application for a low-income housing opportunity. The form was fairly complicated and the agency had a history of rejecting anything that wasn't filled out perfectly; it was a one-shot type of deal.

I truly was sorry. I really had intended to spend a few hours with Rob and then go home. But one thing had led to another, and an hour of lovemaking had turned into several, and I'd fallen into a blissful sleep. Not at all on-brand for me when it came to how I typically spent time with men. I knew that if I told her I was with Rob she would absolutely lose it, and I didn't have the mental bandwidth to have her scream at me right now. So while I didn't want to lie, I decided that I would just tell something a little truth-adjacent. 'I, uh— wasn't feeling well. I ended up falling asleep and when I woke up I realized I'd overslept.' It was a lame excuse, but she seemed to buy it and she let it go. She was clearly preoccupied with her housing application or she almost certainly would have caught me in my lie. I felt extra guilty, sneaking this by her. We continued working our way through her application and I was glad that I was there to help her; she'd made a few fairly significant mistakes as well as the odd typo. Filling out official paperwork was not Lacey's strong suit; unless she was forging something, in which case she was usually very accurate. Interesting, how sometimes we were so good at doing something in one context and awful in another, even when it required very similar skills. At one point, she went up to get us another coffee.

Rob gently bit my bottom lip, and growled. It made me weak at the knees, and I felt a deep ache within me. I was ready for him. I'd been ready since the first time our hands brushed against each other in the kitchen.

'SASHA!' Lacey yelled at me, and I shook my head, startled back into consciousness. I was still sitting there at the cafe, meant to be helping her work on her form. 'Are you day-dreaming again?' *Wow*, I thought. *Not even a few hours after you left his apartment and you're already daydreaming about this guy.*

'Uh, sorry. I guess I'm still not 100%,' I said. She eyed me suspiciously. We went back to completing her form. It took a while to do all the i's and cross all the t's, but by the end we were both feeling pretty good about how it was looking. Lacey folded the document neatly and sealed it in a large envelope addressed to the agency. I really hoped that it was going to be approved, mainly for her sake but also for mine.

'Come clean, Sasha! I know that you were lying beforehand. You weren't ...... You were with him, Rob—,' she could barely say his name, almost spitting it out. 'Weren't you? Tell me!'

'I was,' I said. I looked down, ashamed that I hadn't had the courage to tell her the truth, that I'd felt the need to lie to my good friend. It hadn't felt good to lie, but worst of all my lie had hurt her, betrayed her trust in me. Given all we'd been through together, the times we'd had each other's backs, this had to have been exceptionally hard for her to take.

'You're like in a relationship with him now or something? Rob, I mean,' said Lacey, doubtfully, twirling a piece of her hair. 'I think that's why you've been so distracted. In fact, I wouldn't be surprised if you're feeling just fine and that's the reason you were late.'

'Well... was it at least... good?' Her mind seemed to take a dirty turn. 'I mean... if you're having that much fun, he has to be a good fuck.'

A smile crept onto my face. 'He's amazing.'

'Tell me all the details!' She demanded.

Usually, I would have. The regular me would tell her every explicit detail of my sexual conquests. The way he moved in bed, how dominant he was, if he talked dirty, what positions he favored. Of course, I'd typically have shared the size of his dick, but I knew she'd first seen that at the same time I did. She just hadn't seen it in action, or how it stood at attention, right before he slid into me. I'd normally have told her all about how he used his tongue until I exploded in an intense orgasm. But with Rob, I kind of wanted to keep this to myself. I began to ache, a low throbbing as I recalled him taking care of me.

Trying not to blush, I gave her a look that I hoped would pass for innocence. It seemed like maybe she hadn't fallen for my little story after all.

'You're blushing. And you won't tell me anything. God, it must be good then. You're keeping him a secret. Maybe I'll meet up with him and find out myself, try him on for a ride.' It wouldn't be the first time we'd shared a guy. In fact, we were firmly in eskimo sister territory by this point, many times over. Sometimes, it had been at the same time. I got the impression that she was angling at this now; she wanted to try what I had, and I knew that she still yearned for my body. But, for once, I didn't want to share. And I was finding myself growing increasingly distant from her.

In any case, I got the distinct impression that Lacey was jealous at the possibility that something was blossoming between Rob and me. This wasn't the first time a man had created a bit of a rift in our friendship. I had gotten used to it, given she and I had effectively been in a long-term relationship and knew there were residual feelings there. We inevitably went through this every time one of us started dating, but she seemed to have these types of feelings more than me. 'It's early days, but I do like him. We're still going to hang out lots, you and I,' I reassured her. 'I just want to spend some time with him too, alone.'

'I guess I'm just sad. This feels different. I'm not sure why but I can sense it. I guess I know deep down that this isn't just a fling for you, even though it's early stages. That there's a strong chance you won't be done with him in a few months, that you won't be available to snuggle up to, to be intimate with during a drunken night out.'

'We can still snuggle, just not like that.'

'You know what I mean. I'm just going to miss you like that, that's all.'

'I reached my arm around her and squeezed her to me. It was nice to be wanted.

'Ugh, it sounds like you really like him,' she said, rolling her eyes. 'I guess if that makes you happy, then I'm okay with it. But if he hurts you I'm coming for him, and he won't know what hit him.'

'I know you will, and I'm pretty sure he knows that too,' I said to Lacey, and gave her a long, warm hug.

After meeting with Lacey I rushed home to get changed for my shift at the grocery store. I yanked off the clothes I'd worn on my walk of shame and replaced them with the unflattering, light blue smocked tunic they made us wear, as well as some stretchy black leggings and a pair of Crocs. I couldn't stand the shoes and thought they were ugly as hell, but I'd found that they were the only options that kept my feet relatively comfortable during my long shift at the store. It's not like anyone was likely to see me in them anyway, wedged in the confines of my checkout station.

And the customers, well, they could be a real treat. Living in a city, I experienced my fair share of regulars that lived nearby, as well as people who were passing through. I found that many of them treated me like less than a person, someone there to complete a transaction for them. I'd had a realisation that in some ways, this is a bit how I'd let men treat me, what I felt I'd come to deserve. Approach me, I'd do the thing they'd want, and then they'd leave—sometimes literally throwing money in my direction. Work, pleasure—sometimes it was all the same. This shift was no different, but luckily it wasn't too eventful. The customers behaved themselves for the most part, eager to get their groceries and head home to whatever chaos awaited them.

"Sasha, I need to talk with you at the end of your shift, before you leave." It was Richard, my supervisor, and he'd just approached my checkout station. I didn't like how he'd appear out of nowhere sometimes and kind of hover over my shoulder while I was helping customers. He was a zit-faced young man-child in his early twenties, and he'd basically been offered this job on a silver spoon because his rich parents owned a chain of these stores here in the city and close by. While he was younger than me by several years, he strutted around like a pompous ass, letting everybody know he was the boss. For goodness' sakes, the guy even had a mug that had some cheesy slogan about how he was the #1 boss—I bet he got it for himself, too. I smirked as I imagined him picking it out at one of those stores that sold all types of items covered in word art. "What about, Richard? Somebody steal all the canned tomatoes again?"

"No. It's not about that. I will see you in my office later on, right at the end of your shift. Don't be late." He was being awfully cryptic and I didn't like it. I wondered what he had to tell me.

In a brief respite from customers during my shift, I took the opportunity to glance down at my phone. *Sasha, what's going on? Can we at least talk?* It was Rob, and I realized I'd never got back to him after rushing out of his house. *Rob, so sorry. Will explain later. Meet me after work?* I sent him the address. *Okay, will be there,* he replied.

Begrudgingly, when I finished my shift and closed up my checkout station, I headed to Richard's cluttered office way at the back of the store. I had no idea what he wanted to see me about. When I got there, he had his feet up in the desk and he was tossing an apple up in the air and catching it again like a baseball while he watched employees and customers go about their grocery business on the cameras. 'Anything exciting happening today, Richard? Catch anybody snatching tampons? Are the eyelashes still locked up?' Sadly, the false eyelashes did need to be locked up. Customers wanting to purchase them had to press a little doorbell button for someone to come and release them. *Free the lashes,* I thought. It amused me and made me a little sad at the same time.

'Well, Sasha. You've been on time every shift this month. And you haven't screwed anything up... that I'm aware of.'

'Let me guess. You want to offer me a pay raise?'

'Haha!' Richard laughed out loud, as if that was a ridiculous notion. I was barely paid above minimum wage as it was. 'You know that's not how this works. I do have a proposition for you, though.'

I didn't like being alone in a room with a man—especially a man with some type of power over me—making those types of word choices. However, I really didn't see Richard as a threat. 'What then?'

'Well, we are going to be hiring a few new people and I was wondering about making you a new hire trainer.'

'What's in it for me, then? Dealing with pesky new hires so you don't have to?' He looked away, and I immediately knew that it was partially true.

'Well, for the time you are actually training people you will receive a slightly higher hourly rate,' he said. 'Not much higher, mind you. But it's still something.'

'How much higher?'

'Like 25 cents an hour. Probably for about ten hours a week during busy periods. What do you think?'

I thought it was a crappy deal, for all the headaches that I was sure came with training new hires. But I wondered if there were any other perks attached, and I could use the money even if it wasn't substantial.

'What else does it involve? Just showing them how to use the cash register and stuff?'

'Yeah, orienting them to the store. Taking them through our policies, the one that HR doesn't cover during their orientation. Having them shadow you for a few shifts, and you shadow them for one or two here and there. And you'll get to be involved in the hiring process as well.'

'As in, I get to decide who we hire?'

'Well, you'd be one of several people including me. But yes.'

'Interesting...,' I said, as I thought about the opportunities this might introduce. 'You know what?' He raised an eyebrow at me, curious, knowing I was equally likely to go either way. 'Count me in. I'd love to have more of an influence on this store.'

'Alright then,' he said, looking relieved. 'Keep an eye out for your paperwork. I'll email you in the next day or so.'

'Great talk, bye Richard,' I said. 'Look back at the screen. Mrs. McClintock is pilfering applesauce on Aisle 5 again.' He swivelled in his char to see that the elderly lady with the angelic smile and immaculate head of blue-rinsed curls was indeed taking jars of applesauce and placing them in her oversized bag that sat in the basket of her motorised scooter. I turned around and headed out the door, satisfied that dealing with that would occupy him for long enough for me to leave before getting caught up in any further conversation. I wouldn't normally turn in a customer for taking something, because in most cases they likely did it out of need rather than want. But I really needed a distraction to get out of there because he would have kept talking for ages. Plus, Mrs. McClintock had been a bitch to me at the checkout the other day. *Alls fair in love and applesauce. Be nice to your service workers*, I thought to myself as I headed to the staff area to clock out.

4

To Get What You Want, You Must Ask

As planned, Rob met me outside of work. When I exited, he was pacing around the strip mall looking agitated and concerned. I'd taken a moment after speaking with my manager to get changed into something other than my uniform. I was a bit embarrassed by the way I looked in it, especially when it tended to be a bit grubby by the end of my shift. And there's no way that I was going to let him see me in Crocs. Changing had taken a good five to ten minutes, which had left him waiting longer than I had anticipated.

I walked towards him. 'Sorry I'm late. Got caught up with something.'

He turned to face me, a look of worry on his face. 'Oh good, you're here. I was beginning to worry that you weren't going to show up. Why did you leave so abruptly before? What's going on?'

'I'm sorry, it was Lacey. I was meant to meet her and I... I lost track of time because of you.'

"I see. She seems to need you for one thing or another fairly frequently.'

'She's my best friend, Rob.'

'A needy one.'

'Listen, she's in a bad housing situation and I needed to help her. She's trying to go somewhere that's not dangerous. Not that I owe you this explanation. Why are you being so salty anyway?'

'There's just something funny about you two. Your relationship.'

'She's my best friend, there's nothing much more to say.'

'Seemed like more than that the night that you were in the hotel, from what I remember."

'You don't remember shit, Rob.'

'I saw enough."

'Oh for goodness sakes. It's not that strange.'

'I don't go around banging my friends. Hey George, hey Steve, let's all get together and play some video games and have a threeway on Friday night. Loser gets to bottom! Yeah, nah. I don't do that with my mates.'

'Listen, it's not like that. I was single at the time and we... we have a past. There have been times that we've fooled around. But there's no need for you to be jealous. She and I are just working through some things in our friendship. It's... complicated.'

'Clearly,' said Rob, sounding unconvinced.

'Look, she's bad enough with this whole situation. She does get a bit jealous and possessive when I'm in relationships. We're working on that. She's working on that. Can you please not start, too? I'm here. With you. By choice.' I put my arm on his shoulder and stood on my tiptoes to kiss him underneath his chin. Begrudgingly, he lowered his chin and kissed me back, and hugged me too.

'I know I probably shouldn't, but for some reason I think I should trust you,' he said, continuing to hold me in his arms.

'I know you probably shouldn't, but I'm glad that you do,' I replied.

Having calmed down from his originally agitated state, Rob suggested we head around to his place for a drink and to come up with a plan for later that evening. We were sitting on the couch thinking of possible options, and I was starting to feel a little frisky with Rob sitting so close to me. I leaned in and gave him a kiss on the cheek, my breasts pressing against his side through my shirt. He turned to kiss me back and our hands started roaming into various areas. One of my hands had migrated to his crotch and I was just starting to rub at it gently when the phone rang. It was Lacey. I pulled my hand away, and in hindsight decided to leave it there; this could be fun. Rob and I looked at each and I said, 'Nothing to hide, I'll put her on speakerphone.' He shrugged and nodded.

'Hey Lace!'

'Hey Sasha! What are you up to?' I looked at Rob and grinned. I would have blushed if Lacey was in the room.

'Oh, just relaxing! I'm here with Rob, you're on speakerphone. We're just figuring out what we want to do this evening.' I continued to rub at his groin while we made eye contact, and felt his pants beginning to tighten.

'Hey Rob! I was just doing the same thing, figured maybe we could all do something together. I was thinking... let's all go to Nate's Bar!' Lacey was excited, she'd been wanting to go back there ever since our last eventful night out. She knew she could score an array of illicit items there. And she and Nate had a history of hooking up; she made no secret of the fact she thought he was hot.

'Sure. Want to come, Rob? It will be fun!'

'Nate's...' he said, thoughtfully. 'Don't think I know it. Oh wait, is that the place down the alleyway in downtown, with the pool tables and the dartboards?'

The bulge in his pants was beginning to grow larger, now, despite his distraction.

'Yep, that's the one! With the sticky floors and the subpar food, you got it.'

"I, uh... I think I'll sit this one out. Should probably do some things around the apartment, and put up an ad for a roommate."

'Come onnn,' I said. 'Don't be so boring! You must come with us!'

'Yes, come on Rob. We'll show you a good time. You can meet some of our friends!'

'I'm not sure that's a good idea.' I was surprised that he hadn't jumped at the chance in the first place; he seemed social and had stories about places he'd visited, many of which were dive bars. *Weird,* I thought, but I let it go.

I unzipped his pants and ran my fingers inside his pants. I wrapped fingers firmly around his shaft and began to rub up and down. 'Please, Rob? It would be so nice if you could come. I really think you should consider it.'

He looked at me, as I leant over and licked at the tip of his hardness, just for a moment.

'Well?' Lacey's voice came through the speaker of the phone. We'd both almost forgotten she was there.

'Okay, yes, I'll come,' said Rob.

'Great! Okay, gotta go. Meet you there at 630, Lace.'

'See you!'

I made sure I'd hung up the phone properly, to avoid any subsequent embarrassment, and proceeded to give Rob quite a phenomenal moment on the couch, if I do say so myself. My hands and tongue caressed his manhood as he became increasingly aroused, until he finally couldn't hold it in any longer. 'God, that was incredible. It's really hard to say no to you when you ask questions while doing that, you know?'

'Oh I know,' I said, smiling sweetly.

Nate's was busy as usual, regulars packed along the stools that lined the bar. It was the poster child for a grubby dive bar. The floors were sticky, every surface seemingly coated with some type of questionable substance. Drinks were basic; no craft cocktails or beers from microbreweries here. The signature drink was a beer and a shot. Food options entailed small packets of potato chips or dubious-looking nuggets heated up in a dirty-looking microwave, which sat under a sign that said 'Eat here at your own Risk'. You were liable to get kicked out of the bar for ordering anything more complicated than a vodka soda, and even ordering something like that would result in sideways glances from the regulars lining the bar, and an eye roll from Nate or the other bartender who occasionally picked up a shift.

The bathrooms were filthy and looked like they hadn't been cleaned since the place opened. People had affixed all sorts of stickers covered in everything from insults to band names and logos all over the walls and the mirror. Etched into the wooden cubicles were initials of people who had probably hooked up in there over the years, probably including Lacey's—no shame at all, just facts. Profound quotes and life advice was written in Sharpie. The room smelled heavily of pee and other odors that were difficult to pinpoint.

Two pool tables sat, usually unused, off to the side. They were covered in ring marks from drinks placed on top, as well as the odd cigarette burn. The majority of the pool cues were broken, the type that seemed like you could get a splinter from just looking at them.

Nate's was an acquired taste, but it held plenty of good memories for both me and Lacey, and we found ourselves

returning time and time again. It was never a dull night at
Nate's, and there was always something interesting going on.

Eclectic music blared from the system; metal one song,
oldies the next. Nate looked up from making a half-assed
attempt at wiping down the bar when we entered, and a few
regulars swiveled their necks to look at us as well.

"Look what the cat dragged in," he said, eyes glancing between us and then landing on Lacey.

"You going to drag my cat in later, Nate?" She asked, smiling provocatively at him. There was absolutely no subtlety
between these two. He winked back at her suggestively. "If
you're lucky I'll do more than that, love," he said.

"What'll it be? Cash only, remember."

"Crap, I forgot cash," I whispered.

"I've got it," said Rob.

We each ordered a beer and a shot of whiskey, which Nate
promptly served. Three seats opened up at the bar right then
and we took them.

Rob got up to use the restroom.

"Who's that guy, then?" Asked one of the regulars, turning
to look in his direction as he walked off towards the back
of the room where the restrooms are located. The regular
looked rough, with a pock-marked face that sported a prominent grey-white moustache, arms covered in prison tattoos
poking out from under his shirt.

"Why you asking?" Asked Lacey, defensively. She was
paranoid about giving any sort of personal information to
strangers, probably because she knew what she sometimes
did herself when she had access to that sort of thing. Her
protectiveness on this topic extended to her friends.

"Eh, looks familiar," he said, and swivelled back to face his
drink, which he continued to nurse in his knotted hand.

We had a fun night, enjoying a few more beer and whiskey
shots while we relaxed and people-watched contentedly from
our barstools. A couple of times I noticed people turn around

to look at Rob, but didn't think much of it. They were nosy in here and Rob didn't seem to have been here many times, if at all. They were probably wondering who the new guy with us was. Nosy bastards. At one point we found ourselves dancing sloppily to random songs that played through the janky speakers. As the bar quietened down, Nate at one point came out from behind the bar and slow danced with Lacey, groping her on the ass while they swayed to the music.

"I'm, uh— going to stay here. You guys go!"

"You sure, Lace?"

"Yep yep! I'll be more than fine, once Nate gets done with me. Hahahaha!" She looked at Nate and laughed, almost dropping her purse.

"Okay, if you're sure. Text me in the morning," I said. Nate and I grabbed our coats and headed out the door, ready to spend some quality time at his place.

He nibbled on my ear lobe and it sent tingly sensations screaming through my body. He always seemed to know what I liked. But, I was still craving something more. As gentle as he was, I missed the roughness, the angles that I associated with men. And while I didn't want him to stop doing the things he did, I wanted to explore our boundaries further, for him to be more dominant, exert more control. I didn't want to say I was being pleased too much, but it took a lot of getting used to, being put first, being taken care of, given I was more accustomed to being used by men for their pleasure.

I felt like it was something I needed to talk to him about. Even though it seemed like a small thing, it was blowing up in my mind and I could tell that I was about to sabotage myself by doing something really dumb. I liked this guy, and it felt like I was going to break up with him—or at least slow things way down—because he spent too much time going down on me and not enough being a selfish asshole. I really did need my head checked.

I took a deep breath. 'So... this is going really well, and I don't want to fuck it up.'

'But... I sense a but,' he said. He looked a bit concerned.

'You don't have to be so gentle with me, I know. I mean, I like it from time to time. But I'd also like it if you took charge a bit more.'

'I just didn't want to overstep my bounds. And you should be careful what you ask for.'

'Should I really, though? What do I need to be careful about?'

'You sure you want to find out? Because I will show you just how rough I can be.'

'Like... how rough?' I hadn't expected him to respond like this.

'I prefer to show rather than tell. And once you get me started, I won't stop.'

With that, Rob threw me over his shoulder and carried me into the bedroom where he threw me down hard onto the mattress. He pressed down on me, lifting my hands over my head and directing me to hold onto the headboard. He leaned over to the side of the bed and I heard him pull something out from underneath; it was a box, from which he removed a thin rope made of something that looked like nylon. Somewhat expertly, he tied me to the bedpost, securing my wrists. 'Is this what you wanted?' I looked at him, trying to figure out where this side of him had come from, so unexpectedly. 'Last chance to go back,' he said. 'I mean it. This can't be undone.'

I nodded at him. 'I don't want to go back.'

We made love again, but this time it was not tender. The gentle, loving attention had been replaced what felt like entirely by an intensity, a rough and boundless need for him to have me, to conquer me. He was so much bigger than me physically, and he used his size to control me, to have me move every which way, to do whatever he pleased.

I found myself pleasuring him using my mouth, seeing my hands were tied up, him thrusting his hips until my eyes watered. He spun me around and plowed into me from behind, penetrating me over and over again while I cried out in a combination of pleasure and good pain. His powerful thrusts sent shock waves throughout my body. Tied up, I just had to let him control me, take me in whichever way he wanted. He moved me at his whim, piercing me at all sorts of different angles. After owning me, and taking what was his, he finally came in a fierce, powerful explosion that made me feel like I was going to split in half. He untied me and lay down on his back, and I looked over at him, dazed in a pleasant I-just-got-fucked-really-hard-and-I-wasn't-expecting-it kind of way.

'Is that what you were looking for?' He asked.

'Right on the money,' I said, feeling very satisfied as I snuggled into the crook of his strong and muscular arm that had just held me down and forced me to do whatever he wanted. It was quickly becoming clear to me that there was not a need of mine that this man didn't appear to be able to meet.

5

UNDER YOU, OVER YOU

The next day, I heard my phone beep and I saw a text from Lacey. *On way to Rob's. Meet me there asap. Urgent.*

What in the world, I thought. Why was my ex-girl-friend-turned-best-friend headed to my boyfriend's house. I could only assume that her jealousy had flared and she wanted to have it out with him again. I was concerned, because when she was extremely upset she could turn violent. I tried calling her but it went straight to voicemail.

Can't talk now. Found something out. Meet me at Rob's NOW. Will wait for you outside if you're quick.

Okay, coming. I quickly tapped out a reply and hit send, then called a car to drive me to Rob's place on the other side of town.

The entire drive there, I wondered what possibly could have led to Lacey racing to Rob's house. She barely knew him, and even if she had learned something about him it seemed strange for her to speak to him rather than coming to see me first. Then again, Lacey's behaviour could be a bit unhinged at times, and it had been more erratic recently as she'd been struggling so much with her chaotic living situation.

I clearly arrived at Rob's just in time. Lacey was jumping around like she was auditioning for the part of Rocky Balboa hopping back and forth on the balls of her feet looking like she was about to throw a one-two air punch, and I could tell she would have taken off up the stairs to his place had she not heard my car pull up.

'Lacey!' I called.

'Hurry up, I'm going in!'

'Wait, what is happening?!' I caught up to her and tried to grab her arm but she was on the loose.

'Follow me. No time to talk. I need to confront your piece of shit boyfriend! I am furious!'

'Please, Lace! Tell me what's going on. We can talk to him together!'

Ignoring me, Lacey raced up the steps to his house and started aggressively banging on the door, causing his door to bounce on the hinges. As I caught up to her, I could hear footsteps approaching. The door swung open and Rob stood there, a confused look on his face. 'Lacey? What are you doing here.' He saw me standing a few feet away. 'And Sasha? What's going on—I thought we were hanging out later.'

'You're an undercover cop!' The words flew out of Lacey's mouth, accusatory and full of venom.

'You're—what?! Is it true?!' I was rattled and very confused by her words. She had a flair for the melodramatic but her accusations were on a whole other level.

Instead of denying it, he sighed. 'You found out? How?'

I stopped them both. 'Wait! Tell me what is going on here!'

'He handcuffed himself to the bed, Sasha. Don't you see? He was trying to entrap us. It was all part of a plan. He thought we were running some kind of dodgy scheme from Nate's bar and he followed us back to the hotel.'

'Why would he handcuff himself to the bench. And naked? I don't understand!'

'Nobody understands why. None of us remember. But that's how he ended up in the hotel room in the first place! Don't you see? He isn't interested in you. He's trying to use us, to go after our 'extensive criminal network' as people like him say. He's just using you, Sasha! You're not good enough for him! He thinks he's way too good for people like us!'

The words stung, and I looked up at Rob hoping he would come to the rescue with some kind of reasonable explanation.

'That's not—' he started to say.

'Don't lie to us, pig,' Lacey spat the words out at him as she grabbed my arm. I glanced back and noticed Rob looking down, but he didn't say a word. She pulled me towards the exit stairs and I followed her, my brain racing to process the exchange I had just witnessed. I'd processed sufficiently, however, to realise the situation was not good, and that Rob and I were likely done for good.

I'd headed straight back to my flat. Lacey had wanted to come with me to make sure I was okay and to debrief on what had just occurred, but I just needed to be by myself. A couple of days went by, and I busied myself with whatever I could find. I'd heard my phone buzz a couple of times but I couldn't bear to look at it and so I let it die, refusing to put it on the charger. I numbed myself with ginormous pepperoni pizza slices, way too much bourbon and a bunch of weed that I'd cobbled together from various stashes around my flat. That, combined with copious amounts of trashy reality TV enabled me to zone out, to not focus on what had just transpired.

Despite my focus on busying myself, I called out of work as well. I couldn't bear to see Richard's smarmy face, and knew

I was likely to say or do something I'd regret later. Better to avoid it altogether entirely. He was annoyed when I called, but I'm a good liar. Made up some excuse about my mother needing my help with something urgently. He didn't need to know I hadn't spoken with my mother in over a decade. Might as well make her useful to me now in some way, I figured.

A couple of days after the accusations had flown at Rob's house, I heard a knock on my door. It was Lacey.

I let her in and she immediately started on another verbal rampage. 'I can't believe he'd do that to you, the scumbag! Treating women this way. Lying to you, betraying you! Just an absolutely tragic, lying, asshole of a scumbag!'

I laughed shallowly. 'Sounds like he thinks of *us* as the scumbags, based on what you said.'

'Better a scumbag than a cop. Imagine being a cop and lying about it. That's way, way worse! But if I was one, I'd lie about it, too!' she laughed, bitterly.

'Anyways, I don't want to talk about anything serious. So can you please stop? Distract me with something fun.'

She spent the rest of the day hanging out with me, trying to make me laugh and cracking bad jokes. We walked over to the gas station and giggled in the aisles as we picked out random snacks to take back to my flat. Hours went by. It felt fun and carefree, just being with Lacey with no obligations, and thoughts of Rob left my mind while I just enjoyed being with my friend.

'Hey,' I said, looking over at Lacey. She glanced back in my direction as I said, 'You need a place to stay for the night?'

'Yeah, if you don't mind. Shit's going down back at the group house. You know how Tony gets. It's not really safe right now, and there's no chance in hell I'd get any sleep.' Tony played some type of lead role at the group house. He had a reputation for becoming volatile when he drank, which was often. Lacey had a strong lock on her door but she still needed to leave to go to one of the common areas every now and then, and there were often multiple strangers in various states of consciousness on the couch, on the floor, helping themselves to items from the refrigerator.

'We've got to get you out of there soon, Lace. I'm worried about you.'

'Don't I know it.'

'What happened with your application? You got it in on time, right?'

'Yes. Still waiting to hear back. I'm not sure how long it's going to take, anywhere between a couple of days and a few weeks. Nerve-racking waiting to hear.'

It was hard to reestablish yourself after being inside. Nobody wanted to take a chance on you ducking out on them without paying for something, no matter how big or small. No credit, no guarantors, no income. It was hard to find a place to live, or a company who would hire you. There were programs out there that offered to help, but Lacey was proud and usually found they came with some sort of catch—too religious, too interfering. Hell, I'd been in the same boat and only lucked out with my job because the friend of an old high school buddy took pity on me and offered me a job at the discount grocery store. Lacey hadn't been so lucky and, while I knew the answer wasn't to let her sleep on my couch every night, I felt like it was my responsibility to help her get on her feet so she could start really living. The low-income housing program she'd applied for was highly competitive, but if she was successful with her application it seemed like it would be a good start to get her on the right track.

'By the way, whose the asshole with spaghetti on his shirt that's knocking on people's doors all over the flat complex?'

'Oh that's Eugene, he's the property manager and a grade A creep. So basically he's here on behalf of the landlord. Goodness knows why they hired him.'

'Yeah, I could tell he was a creep by the way he stared at my ass. Almost decked him. Asked him if he had eyes for

Christmas, and he just kept looking. He'd better keep out of both of our ways.'

'Yep. I just try to pay my rent on time and stay as far away from him as possible. If your application goes through, I hope you're spared the joy of a landlord like Eugene,' I said, and we both laughed.

Eventually, we both drifted off to sleep, my apartment festooned with snack wrappers, beer cans and liquor bottles.

I woke up the next day, for once knowing exactly where I was. I had an early shift at the grocery store, though, so I saw Lacey out and headed to work.

Time flew by during my shift as customer after customer came through. 'Thank you for stopping at Pack for Less, have a nice day.' 'Thank you for stopping by, please come again.' I was like a robot, automated, going through the motions like the well-oiled checkout chick I had become. The job was boring as shit, but it was easy too, and it paid the bills. They'd offered me a promotion to assistant manager at one point, but I had no interest in running around after the zitty teenagers who worked alongside me and always had some sort of drama going on. I just liked to show up and do my thing, and get the hell out of there as soon as clockout time rolled around. I was still surprised at myself for accepting the new hire trainer opportunity, but that didn't start for another month or so and I was still considering changing my mind.

'Sasha!' The sound of my name was jarring. I wasn't used to anyone except for my jerk of a manager using it at work. I looked up, startled. To my surprise, it was Rob.

'Rob! What in the world are you doing here?' It was strange to see him here, out of context. This was my space, my environment where I could be relatively invisible and check my mind out while I checked people out. I felt annoyed that my little cone of privacy had been infiltrated, and I was still a bit grumpy at Rob which didn't help matters.

'You live on the other side of town, in a much nicer neighbourhood than this. I'm guessing you're not here for the almond milk special.'

'I need to talk to you, Sash. And you haven't been returning my calls.'

'Well as you can see, I'm very busy,' I said, gesturing at the line behind him that was growing longer by the second. People were starting to glare and tap their feet angrily as it was clear that he was not there to buy anything.

'Just give me a moment.'

'Customers are waiting, Rob. Let me get back to work.'

'Here—I'll buy something. Just give me a second.' He grabbed a few packs of orange-flavoured gum from the little dispenser in front of the checkout and tossed them gently onto the conveyor belt. 'Ring me up. I just need one minute.'

I sighed and glanced down at the line, shrugging in apology. People seemed to have calmed down slightly seeing that the rude customer in front of them was actually buying something, not just chatting up the checkout girl.

I rang up his gum while he continued to talk. 'Sasha, please. I can explain everything. Just give me the opportunity to explain. Do you have a break coming up soon? Or when do you get off work? I just need to talk to you, please.'

'That'll be three-fifty.' He handed me cash. 'And my break is in ten minutes. Come and meet me by the door at the back of the store. Don't be late, they're militant about time here.'

'I'll be there,' he said. 'Thank you. This is important.' I handed him his receipt and he walked away. I was relieved for the moment, to be able to go back to once again focusing on the *beep beep beep* sound as I checked out the steady stream of customers.

I opened the door behind me and pulled him into the dark storage cupboard.

Without reflecting on why we were there, the opportunity to be alone with him, here, overcame me. It felt forbidden, a little naughty. This was one of the rooms that creepy Richard couldn't see on his maze of cameras, and this felt like giving the entitled little man child the middle finger which was a very enjoyable feeling. My anger at Rob quickly transformed into desire and I pulled him to me in a passionate kiss, my tongue caressing his. He didn't resist, and pulled me to him, hand on the small of my back.

I reached my arm down and rubbed at the fabric of his jeans, through to where I felt a bulge forming in his pants.

'I missed you,' he said, breathless.

'I missed you as well.'

I got to my knees, unbuttoning and unzipping his jeans and pulling down his pants and underwear, and began to pleasure him with my mouth. Seriously, it was some of my best work. In the dark, dingy storage cupboard of the Pack for Less.

As he moved back and forth against me, I used my tongue and my hands to bring him to ecstasy. His body tensed as he climaxed, while I knelt there on the floor. I stood up, very pleased with myself. 'Weren't expecting that, were you?'

He looked surprised but also very satisfied. 'Ah, no—that is definitely not what I was expecting.'

'I'm still fucking furious at you, by the way. But you're still sexy as hell. I needed a little excitement on my break'

'What time are you off?'

'Five-thirty,' I said. 'Wait for me? We really do need to talk.'

We emerged from the storage closet as Rob finished buttoning up his pants, resulting in a curious look from a little old lady pushing her cart right past us right at the time we emerged. As we walked to the front of the store, I saw Richard emerging from the side of the aisle. 'Go!' I hissed at Rob. 'Meet you outside after my shift!' 'Sasha, you know how we feel about having acquaintances visit during our shifts.'

'Oh, sorry Richard—he's leaving right away. It was my break and, uh—I'm just so proud of working here. I wanted to give him a tour around the store, show him what amazing work we do under your leadership.'

'Oh, I see,' he said, rubbing his chin thoughtfully as I headed back to my checkout station and flipped the light on to indicate I was once again open for business.

I'd been in denial for several days, and had tried to block everything out. But as I stood there, processing checkout items for the remainder of the shift, my mind went off on its own path ready to process everything that had happened. I found myself in a moment of clarity. All of a sudden, everything made sense. His crash pad, his secrecy. The way that some of the regulars had recognised him that night at Nate's dive bar, but couldn't quite put their finger on it. I felt hurt and deceived, but part of me also realized that it's hardly something he could have just come out and told me. We hadn't even known each other for very long, and this was a big secret. He didn't know if I'd use it against him, and it's information that could really have hurt him, and his career. To be fair, I'd kept secrets from him as well. It's not like I went up to him, extended my arm for a handshake and simultaneously produced my rap sheet so he could peruse my extensive criminal record. If he was trying to get information from Lacey or me, he was going to be sorely disappointed. Except for the odd small-time hustle that Lacey got involved in, and hanging

out with some minor players in petty theft rings, we were for
the most part on the up-and-up. Some secrets are meant to
be kept until they're ready to tell. So while I didn't like his
dishonesty by omission, and felt uncomfortable at the fact he
was a cop, there was a sliver of understanding somewhere
inside of me.

As planned, I met him outside the grocery store at the end
of my shift. Once again, he was pacing around the strip mall
looking agitated and very serious.

'I'm so sorry. I was trying to find a way to tell you. I think
it's better if we talk back at my place.' I agreed to head back
with him and we drove in silence. I tried to formulate the
words I wanted and needed to say, and hoped hard that he
wasn't going to drop any more explosive info on me. When
we reached his apartment, we took a seat on his couch and
sat there, looking at each other.

'So you were looking down on me, trying to use me for my
connections?' I had to ask him, because that's certainly how it
felt.

'At first, yes. But that's before I knew you, Sasha. It was
just work I knew that Lacey was for sure all tied up in some
weird scheme, and I wasn't sure if you were involved. That's
why I originally got close, to find out. But I quickly developed
feelings for you. First, I''l admit, it was entirely physical,
because you're fucking sexy. But then, the more we hung out
I realized I actually like you... I really like you.'

'You... like like me?' I asked.

'You know what I mean. And I know you're not involved in
anything bad. I just want to be around you.'

'How did you end up handcuffed to the bed, anyway? And naked?'

'I honestly don't know,' Rob said. We both laughed. 'We were all having a drink and then I woke up like that.'

'Wow.'

'Yeah, I'd say it was a night to remember, but nobody can remember it.'

'Is someone in your line of work even allowed to hang around with the likes of me? Someone with an extensive criminal past and a record to prove it?'

'I mean, I'll have to fill out some paperwork. But you're more than worth it,' he said, pulling my chin up so that our mouths met, engaging me in a deep kiss.

'How worth it?' I asked, noticing that his pants were beginning to stretch tight across his front. 'You going to show me how much you still want to be with me?'

'Am I ever,' he grinned, and pulled me by my hand to the bedroom.

He lifted me up so that I was straddling him and he kissed me, long and deep, his tongue interlocked with mine, and I could feel his erection pressing against me. I could tell that I was growing extremely wet by the intense throbbing sensation between my legs. He reached down and unbuttoned himself and I clung to him with my arms and my legs while he pulled down his jeans and underwear, freeing his girth. My panties were the only thing in the way so I pulled them to the side and, still standing, I pressed myself down and he slid into me. I rhythmically moved my hips and we moved against each other, kissing, his strong arms wrapped around me as he moved inside of me. My heart pounded in my chest as the emotions from the previous few days flooded through me. As he moved towards the bed and placed me on my back he once again slid inside me and began to penetrate deep into my core. We rode together and I felt tears sliding down my cheeks—the stress and the joy, the happiness and the hurt, the betrayal and the tiny sparks that had the potential to explode into real love, all bubbling to the surface. As he rubbed against me and inside me, I found my body tense up and little explosions go off, causing pleasure to radiate throughout my body; moments later, I felt his body do the same in response to my own. We lay in each other's arms, drained, satisfied, angry, understanding, lost, happy. And most of all, relieved that we could also tell our truths, and wanted each other regardless. We still had a lot to talk about, but this was a good start.

'So you've decided to stay with him then? Even though he lied to you, betrayed you?' Lacey looked at me, skeptically. I'd asked her to come and meet me at the coffee shop where we'd prepared her housing application.

'He had to keep his cover for a while, you know. To make sure he could trust me.'

'Keep his cover... look at you, sounding like a cop now.' She smirked at me.

'Lacey, I know this is hard for you, but he came clean. It's not easy for him, you know. It's created complications for him at his work. He said he needed to fill out some paperwork and that it would be okay, but I know it's had more of an impact than that. They'll be questioning his judgment. It might even threaten his promotion prospects. Knowing he's involved with a dirty ex-con.'

'Oh no, he won't be able to become an even bigger cop? Bring out the tiny violins.'

'Lace, you're not being very understanding. Can you please just let me give this a shot, without you trying to tank it before it even started. I'm begging you.'

Lacey looked at me, searchingly, and my words must have rung true because she grabbed my hand, interlocking it in hers and said, 'I'll do my best. Until he messes with you, and then I promise with everything in my being, I will do my worst.'

'Thank you for having my back.'

'Always.' She pulled me into a hug.

'And what about us, our friendship? It's been a bit messed up for the past few weeks. I know you've been annoyed at me but things have just been weird between us. I know we go through phases where we bicker, but this feels like something more, something that could be permanent.

'It's just been really hard seeing with you that someone you like so much. I'm used to being the closest person to you, you know? And with the type of men you've been in relationships since we've got out, you've needed me more. A shoulder to cry on, someone to vent to—hell, someone to get wasted with and wake up naked next to. But you don't need me for those things anymore. It's been hard letting you go.'

'You're still so very important to me, Lacey. And friendships change over time, they evolve. I'm sure you can forgive me for not continuing to date absolute pieces of trash so that you can make me feel better about it.'

'I guess I can forgive you. Rather that than having you fall out of my life completely.'

'Speaking of which, did you find out about your application yet?'

'Oh my gosh, I was so wrapped up in talking about Rob that I forgot to tell you—yes, and it was accepted! I'm in! I can move in next month.'

'I'm so pleased for you, Lacey! Really. This is going to be the start of big things for you, I'm sure of it. Your silver lining is coming.' I hugged her, and she beamed, proud to have a safe place to call home in her very near future.

I didn't mention that I'd accepted the new hire trainer role at the store because I'd have some sway in who we hired. I wanted to make sure everything panned out the way I was hoping it would. Next on my list was helping her get a decent job. It'd no doubt drive me nuts having her around me that many hours in a day, but it seemed like the right thing to do.

Lacey looked over at me. 'Can you just promise me one thing, though, Sasha?'

'What's that?'

'That next time we wake up and there's a hot naked man handcuffed inside our cheap hotel room, he's mine?'

I laughed. 'It's a deal.'

THE END

ABOUT AUTHOR

Heidi Stark is a romance novelist who enjoys traveling (preferably staying in non-seedy motel rooms), great food and even better friendships. She'd be lost without ice cream, her cats, and of course a good book to curl up with.

ALSO BY HEIDI STARK

More books coming soon. Stay tuned.

A SUSPENSEFUL ROMANCE

LOVE

in a seedy

motel room

HEIDI STARK

Made in the USA
Middletown, DE
22 September 2023

39082213R00047